Good Times at the Lake

By Christine Economos
Illustrated by Janice Skivington

Copyright © 2000 Metropolitan Teaching and Learning Company.
Published by Metropolitan Teaching and Learning Company.
Printed in the United States of America.
All rights reserved. No part of this publication may be reproduced or utilized in any form or by any means, electronic or mechanical, including photocopying, recording, or by any information storage or retrieval system without permission in writing from the publisher. For information regarding permission, write to Metropolitan Teaching and Learning Company, 33 Irving Place, New York, NY 10003.

ISBN 1-58120-031-5

2 3 4 5 6 7 8 9 CL 02 01 00

Nina said, "Take a ride to the lake with us.
Grab a bag and tell your mom, Ben."

Ben said, "It isn't that bad, Nina. See how good Mop is on my lap. She just has a fit when she gets a bath."

Mom said, "You can all have a swim.
But Mop can't.
She can sit by me."

Dad said, "Mop likes to be with us.
We will all get in the van.
When she sees us go, she will come."

Ben said, "We had a good time. But Mop had a better time than we did.
She had a swim and a bath.
And she did not have a fit."